Goldwin Smith

An Inaugural Lecture

SALZWASSER
VERLAG

Goldwin Smith

An Inaugural Lecture

Reprint of the original, first published in 1859.

1st Edition 2022 | ISBN: 978-3-37512-168-6

Verlag (Publisher): Salzwasser Verlag GmbH, Zeilweg 44, 60439 Frankfurt, Deutschland
Vertretungsberechtigt (Authorized to represent): E. Roepke, Zeilweg 44, 60439 Frankfurt, Deutschland
Druck (Print): Books on Demand GmbH, In de Tarpen 42, 22848 Norderstedt, Deutschland

AN

INAUGURAL LECTURE

DELIVERED BY

GOLDWIN SMITH, M.A.,

REGIUS PROFESSOR OF MODERN HISTORY IN THE UNIVERSITY OF OXFORD.

NOVEMBER, MDCCCLIX.

1859

Oxford and London:

J. H. AND JAS. PARKER.

AN INAUGURAL LECTURE, &c.

NEW Statutes having just been made by the Crown, on the recommendation of the Council, for the purpose of adapting the Professorship I have the honour to hold to the present requirements of the University, this seems a fit occasion for saying a few words on the study of Modern History in Oxford, and the functions of this Chair in relation to that study. I made some remarks on the subject in commencing my first course with my class; but the new statutes were then only under consideration, and before venturing to address the University, I wished to see something of the state of the Modern History school, and the duties of my Chair.

This Chair was founded in the reign of George I., and its original object was to train students for the public service. The foundation was double, one Chair here and one at Cambridge. Attached to each Chair were two teachers of modern languages, and twenty King's scholars, whose education in history and the modern languages the Professor was to superintend; and the most proficient among whom he was to recommend from time to time for employment, at home or abroad, in the service of the State. Diplomacy was evidently the first object of the foundation, for a knowledge of treaties is mentioned in the letters patent of foundation as specially necessary' for the public interest. Some subsequent regulations, though of doubtful validity, named International Law and Political Economy, with the method of reading Modern History and Political Biography, as the subjects for the Professor's lectures. Thus the whole foundation may be said to have been in great measure an anticipation of the late resolution of the University to found a school of Law and Modern History. The Professorship of Modern History, the Professorship of Political Economy, the Chichele Professorship of Diplomacy, the Professor and Teachers of the Modern Languages, do now for the students of our present school just what the Professor of History and his two teachers of Modern Languages were originally intended to do for the twenty King's scholars under their care. The whole of these subjects have further been brought into connection, in the new school, with their natural associate, the study of Law.

I have failed, in spite of the kind assistance of my friends, the Librarian of the Bodleian and the Keeper of the Archives, to trace the real author of what we must allow to have been an enlightened and far-sighted scheme—a scheme which, had it taken effect, might have filled the Parliament and the public service of the last century with highly-trained legislators and statesmen, and perhaps have torn some dark and disastrous pages from our history. It is not likely that the praise is due to the King himself, who, though not without sense and public spirit, was indifferent to intellectual pursuits. Conjecture points to Sir Robert Walpole. That Minister was at the height of power when the Professorship was founded under George I. When the foundation was confirmed under George II., he had just thrust aside the feeble pretensions of Sir Spencer Compton, and gathered the reins of government, for a moment placed in the weak hands of the favourite, again into his own strong and skilful grasp. If Walpole was the real founder, if he even as minister approved the foundation, it is a remarkable testimony from a political leader of a turn of mind practical to coarseness, and who had discarded the literary statesmen of the Somers and Halifax school, to the value of high political education as a qualification for the public service. It is also creditable to the memory of a minister, the reputed father of the system of Parliamentary corruption, that he should have so far anticipated one of the best of modern reforms as to have been willing to devote a large amount of his patronage to merit, and to take that merit on the recommendation of Universities, one of which, at least, was by no means friendly to the Crown.

King George I., however, or his Minister, was not the first of English rulers who had endeavoured to draw direct from the University a supply of talented and highly-educated men for the service of the State. I almost shrink from mentioning the name which intrudes so grimly into the long list of the Tory and High Church Chancellors of Oxford. But it was at least the nobler part of Cromwell's character which led him to protect Oxford and Cambridge from the levelling fanaticism of his party, to make himself our Chancellor, to foster our learning with his all-pervading energy, and to seek to draw our choicest youth to councils which it must be allowed were always filled, as far as the evil time permitted, with an eye to the interest of England and to her interest alone. Cromwell's name is always in the mouths of those who despise or hate high education, who call, in every public emergency, for native energy and rude common sense,—for no subtle and fastidious philosophers, but strong practical men. They seem to think that he really was a brewer of Huntingdon who left his low calling in a fit of fanatical enthusiasm to lead a great cause (great, whether it were the right cause or the wrong,) in camp and council, to win Dunbar against a general who had foiled Wallenstein, to fascinate the imagination of Milton, and by his administration at home and abroad to raise England, in five short years and on the morrow of a bloody civil war, to a height of greatness to which she still looks back with a proud and wistful eye. Cromwell, to use his own words, "was by birth a gentleman, living neither in any considerable height, nor yet in obscurity;" he was educated, suitably to his birth, at a good classical school; he was at Cambridge; he read law; but what was much more than this, he, who is supposed to have owed his power to ignorance and narrowness of mind, had brooded almost to madness over the deepest questions of religion and politics, and, as a kinsman of Hampden and an active member of Hampden's party, had held intimate converse on those questions with the profoundest and keenest intellects of that unrivalled age. And therefore his ambition, if it was treasonable, was not low. Therefore he bore himself always not as one who gambled for a stake, but as one who struggled for a cause. Therefore the great soldier loved the glory of peace above the glory of war, and the moment he could do so, sheathed his victorious sword; therefore, if he was driven to govern by force, he was driven to it with reluctance, and only after long striving to govern by nobler means; therefore he kept a heart above tinsel, and, at a height which had turned the

head of Cæsar, remained always master of himself;
therefore he loved and called to his council-board
high and cultivated intellect, and employed it to
serve the interest of the State without too anxiously
enquiring how it would serve his own; therefore he
felt the worth of the Universities, saved them from
the storm which laid throne and altar in the dust, and
earnestly endeavoured to give them their due place
and influence as seminaries of statesmen. Those who
wish to see the conduct of a real brewer turned into
a political chief should mark the course of Santerre
in the French Revolution. Those who wish to see
how power is wielded without high cultivation and
great ideas, should trace the course of Napoleon,
so often compared with Cromwell, and preferred to
him;—of Napoleon the great despiser of philosophers;—and ask whether a little of the philosophy
which he despised might not have mitigated the
vulgar vanity which breathes through his bulletins,
and tempered his vulgar lust of conquest with some
regard for nobler things. It would indeed be a flaw
in nature if that which Arnold called the highest
earthly work, the work of government, were best performed by blind ignorance and headlong force, or by a
cunning which belongs almost as much to brutes as
man. The men who have really left their mark on
England, the founders of her greatness from Alfred to
the Elizabethan statesmen, and from the Elizabethan
statesmen down to Canning and Peel, have been cultivated in various ways; some more by study, some
more by thought; some by one kind of study, some
by another: but in one way or other they have been
all cultivated men. The minds of all have been fed
and stimulated, through one channel or other, with

the great thoughts of those who had gone before them ; and prepared for action by lofty meditations, the parents of high designs.

The attempt of the Crown, however, to found a political school at Oxford and Cambridge by means of this Professorship, must be said, at the time, to have failed. Perhaps at Oxford the Whig seed fell on a Jacobite soil. Long after this the evils of a disputed succession were felt here, and the University was the slave of one of the two political factions, to the utter loss of her true power and her true dignity as the impartial parent of good and great citizens for the whole nation. The Jacobite Hearne has recorded in his Diary his anguish at the base condescension of the Convocation in even returning thanks for the Professorship to the royal founder, whom he styles " the Duke of Brunswick, commonly called King George I." Nor does the new study in itself seem to have been more welcome, at this time, than other innovations. The Convocation point their gratitude especially to that part of the royal letter which promises " that the hours for teaching His Majesty's scholars the Modern Languages shall be so ordered, as not to interfere with those already appointed for their academical studies." What the academical studies were which were to be so jealously guarded against the intrusion of Modern History and Modern Languages, what they were even for one who came to Oxford, gifted, ardent, eager to be taught, is written in the autobiography of Gibbon. It is written in every history, every essay, every novel, every play which describes or betrays the manners of the clergy and gentry of England in that dissolute, heartless, and unbelieving age. It is written in the still darker records of faction, misgovernment, ini-

quity in the high places both of Church and State,
and in the political evils and fiscal burdens which
have been bequeathed by those bad rulers even to our
time. The corruption was not universal, or the nation
would never have lifted its head again. The people
received the religion which the gentry and clergy
had rejected: the people preserved the traditions of
English morality and English duty: the people re-
paired, by their unflagging industry, the waste of pro-
fligate finance, and of reckless and misconducted wars.
But as to the character of the upper classes, whose
educational discipline the Convocation of that day
were so anxious to guard against the intrusion of
new knowledge, there cannot be two opinions. We
have left that depravity far behind us, but in the
day of its ascendancy perhaps its greatest source was
here.

But not only was Oxford lukewarm in encouraging
the new studies; the Crown, almost unavoidably,
failed to do its part. At the time of the foundation
Walpole was all-powerful, and might have spared a
part of the great bribery fund of patronage for the
promotion of merit. But soon followed the fierce
Parliamentary struggles of his declining hour, when
the refusal of a place in a public office might have
cost a vote, a vote might have turned a division, and
an adverse division might not only have driven the
hated minister from place, but have consigned him to
the Tower. After the fall of Walpole came a long
reign of corruption, connived at, though not shared,
even by the soaring patriotism of Chatham, in which
it would have been in vain to hope that anything
which could be coveted by a boroughmonger would
be bestowed upon a promising student. Under these

most adverse circumstances, few King's Scholars seem ever to have been appointed. The Scholars, and the commission given by the original statutes to the Professor to recommend the most diligent for employment under the Crown, have now, after long abeyance, been formally abolished by the Council in framing the new statutes; I confess, a little to my regret. The abuse of patronage drove the nation to the system of competitive examination. Competitive examination, in its turn, may be found to have its drawbacks. In that case, there may be a disposition to try honest recommendation by public bodies; and in that event, it might not have been out of place for the Universities to remind the Government of the expressed desire and the old engagement of the Crown.

In the meantime, Modern History and its associate studies enjoy the more certain encouragement of a Modern History School and academical honours. They also enjoy, or ought to enjoy, the encouragement of being the subjects of examination for the Fellowships of All Souls; a College destined, by the Statesman who founded it, in great measure for the study of the Civil Law, that study which once formed the Statesmen of Europe and connected the Universities with the cabinets of Kings, and the wealthy and powerful professors of which, in Italy, its most famous seat, sleep beside great princes, magistrates, and nobles, in many a sumptuous tomb.

Possibly, also, the School of Law and Modern History being practically a modified revival of the Faculty of Law in the University, the subjects of examination for the degree of B.C.L., and the qualifications for the degree of D.C.L. might be modified in a corresponding manner. If this were done, I should not despair of seeing a real value imparted to these degrees. I would commend this point to the consideration of the Council.

The University seems to have had two objects in instituting the New Schools, that of increasing industry by bringing into play the great motive power of love of a special subject, and that of making education a more direct training for life. These are the titles of the History School to continued support, even if its state for some time to come should need indulgence; as indulgence I fear it will long need, unless the University should see fit to place it under more regular and authoritative guidance, and unless the difficulties which Colleges find in providing permanent tuition in this department, can be in some way overcome.

That the love of a special subject is a great spur to industry, needs no proof; and it has never yet been shewn that the mind is less exercised when it is exercised with pleasure. Every experienced student knows that the great secret of study is to read with appetite. Under the old system, the University relied mainly on the motive of ambition. Such ambition is manly and generous, and its contests here, conducted as they are, teach men to keep the rules of honour in the contests of after life. Study pursued under its influence generally makes an aspiring character; but study pursued, in part, at least, from love of the subject, makes a happier character; and why should not this also be taken into account in choosing the subjects of education? But the grand and proved defect of ambition as a motive is, that it fails with most natures, and that it fails especially with those, certainly not the least momentous part of our charge, whose position as men of wealth and rank is already fixed for them in life.

To make University education a more direct preparation for after life, may be called Utilitarianism. The objection, no doubt, flows from a worthy source. We are the teachers of a great University, and we may take counsel of her greatness. We may act, and are bound to act, on far-sighted views of the real interests of education, without paying too much deference to the mere fashion of the hour. But the most far-sighted views of the real interests of education would lead us to make our system such as to draw hither all the mental aristocracy of the country ; its nobility, its gentry, its clergy, its great professions, the heads of its great manufactures and trades. It was so in the earlier period of our history, when almost every man of intellectual eminence in any line must have looked back to the Universities not only as the scene of his youth but as the source of the knowledge which was to him power, wealth, and honour. To power, wealth, and honour, our system of education must lead, if it is to keep its hold on England, though it should be to power which shall be nobly used, to wealth which shall be nobly spent, and to honour which shall shine beyond the hour. Utilitarianism in education is a bad thing. But the great places of national education may avoid Utilitarianism till Government is in the hands of ambitious ignorance, till the Bench of Justice is filled with pettifoggers, till coarse cupidity and empiricism stand beside the sick bed, till all the great levers of opinion are in low, uneducated hands. Our care for the education of the middle classes, however it may be applauded in itself, will ill compensate the country for our failure to perform thoroughly the task of educating our proper charge, the upper classes, and training them to do, and teaching them how to do, their duty to the people.

There is one class of our students,—I fear of late a diminishing class,—which I believe the University had especially in view in instituting the School of Law and Modern. History, and which it was thought particularly desirable to win to study by the attraction of an interesting subject, and to train directly for the duties of after life; more especially as the education of this class closes here. The duties in after life of the class I refer to are peculiar; and its position seems fast becoming unique in Europe.

"In Flanders, Holland, Friesland," says Mr. Laing in his well-known work on Europe in 1848, "about the estuaries of the Scheldt, Rhine, Ems, Weser, Elbe and Eyder; in a great part of Westphalia and other districts of Germany; in Denmark, Sweden, and Norway; and in the south of Europe, in Switzerland, the Tyrol, Lombardy and Tuscany, the peasants have from very early times been the proprietors of a great proportion of the land. France and Prussia" (it seems he will soon be able to say Russia) "have in our times been added to the countries in which the land is divided into small estates of working peasant proprietors. In every country of Europe, under whatever form of government, however remotely and indirectly affected by the wars and convulsions of the French revolution, and however little the laws, institutions and spirit of the government may as yet be in accordance with this social state of the people, the tendency, during this century, has been to the division and distribution of the land into small estates of a working peasant proprietary, not to its aggregation into large estates of a nobility and gentry. This has been the real revolution in Europe. The only exception is Great Britain." In the colonies, we may add, even of Great Britain, the tendency to small estates and working proprietors prevails ; and as colonies are drawn, generally speaking, from the most advanced and enterprising part of the population, their tendencies are to their mother country a prophecy of her own future.

The force of opinion in this age is paramount ; and it runs with the certainty, if not with the speed of electricity round the sympathetic circle of European nations. Of these two systems, the system of great landowners and the system of small working proprietors, that will assuredly prevail which European opinion shall decide to be the better for the whole people. But which is the better system for the whole people, is a question with a double aspect. One aspect is that of physical condition ; the other is that of civilization. It may be, that the civilizing influence of a resident class of gentry, well educated themselves, and able and willing to be the moral and social educators of the people, may countervail the material advantages which a landowning peasantry enjoy, and even the accession of moral dignity, the prudence, the frugality, which the possession of property in the lower class, even more than in ours, seems clearly to draw in its train. But then the gentry must know their position, and own their duty to those by whose labour they are fed. They must be resident, they must be well-educated, they must be able and willing to act as the social and moral educators of those below them. They must do their part, and their

Universities must make it a definite and primary
object to teach them to do their part, in a system
under which, if they will do their part, they at least
may enjoy such pure, true, and homefelt happiness as
never Spanish grandee or French seigneur knew. If
they are to make it their duty, under the influence
of overstrained notions of the rights of property, to
squander the fruits of the peasant's labour in dull
luxury, or in swelling the vice and misery of some
great capital, the cry already heard, " the great
burden on land is the landlord," may swell till it
prevails; till it prevails in England, as it has pre-
vailed in the land, separated from ours only by a few
leagues of sea, which, eighty years ago, fed the luxury
of Versailles. The luxury of Versailles seemed to
itself harmless and even civilizing; it was graceful
and enlightened; it was not even found wanting in
philanthropy, though it was found wanting in active
duty. Before the Revolution, the fervour and the
austerity of Rousseau had cast out from good society the levity and sensuality of Voltaire[a]. Atheism,
frivolity, heartlessness, sybaritism, had gone out of
fashion with Madame de Pompadour and Madame
Dubarri. Theism, philanthropy, earnestness, even
simplicity of life, or at least the praise of simplicity of
life, had become the order of the day; and the beams
of better times to come played upon the current, and
the rainbow of Utopian hope bent over it, as it drew,
with a force now past mortal control, to the most
terrible gulf in history. Even the genius of Carlyle
has perhaps failed to paint strongly enough this cha-
racteristic of the Revolution, and to make it preach

[a] See Lavallée, Histoire des Français. Bk. iii., section 3,
chap. 5.

clearly enough its tremendous lesson as to the difference between social sentiment and social duty. We
know Paley's apologue of the idle pigeon, consuming,
squandering, scattering about in lordly wastefulness
the store of corn laboriously gathered for him by the
subservient flock. That apologue, catching the eye
of King George III., is said to have cost Paley a
bishopric. But its moral, duly pointed, is nothing
more dangerous than that property has its duties.
Landed property, fortunately for the moral dignity
and real happiness of its possessors, has its obvious
duties. Funded property, and other kinds of accu-
mulated wealth, have duties less obvious to which
the possessors must be guided, if their Universities
desire to see them living the life and holding the
place in creation not of animals of large, varied, and
elaborate consumption, but of men.

But can education teach the rich to do their duty?
If it cannot, why do the rich come to places of education? If it cannot, what have we to do but abdicate
that part of our trust? But experience says it can.
Look round to the really well-educated men of property of your acquaintance. Are they not, as a body,
good and active members of society, promoters of good
social objects, and, if landowners, resident, and endea-
vouring to earn the rent the labour of the people pays
them, by doing good among the people? In feudal
times, when the landed aristocracy and gentry owed
the State military service, they were trained to arms;
now they owe the State social service, and they must
be trained by education to social duties, not to the
duties of schoolmasters, lecturers, or statists, but to
the duties of landed gentlemen. Before the late
changes, the influence of education had hardly been

tried on them. A little philology and a little geome-
try, forgotten as soon as learnt, might sharpen the
wits a little, but could awaken no lasting intellectual
interests, open no intellectual pleasures to compete
with animal enjoyments, kindle generous sympathies
and aspirations in no heart. Now we have for the
aristocracy and gentry a school, in effect of Social
Science, that is, of Jurisprudence, including Constitutional Law, and of Political Economy, with History
illustrating both. This appeals, as directly as it can,
to the interests of the class for whom it was insti-
tuted, and by whom it appears not to be rejected. It
is an experiment, but it is a rational and practical
experiment, and human legislation can be no more.

I dwell on these points because we have heard expressed, by persons of influence in Council and Congre-
gation, a desire, which I doubt not extensively prevails, to undo our recent legislation; a feeling, which
if it does not actually bring us back to the old system, may cripple the operation of the new. The old
system stood condemned, as far as the gentry were
concerned, not by its theoretical imperfections as a
scheme of education, but by its manifest results;
results which are felt and deplored in country pa-
rishes by clergymen who uphold the system here.
History and its cognate subjects may not prove as
much intellectual power as the mixed philosophical
and philological culture of the old Classical school.
Their true place and value, in a perfect system of education, will be fixed, when we shall have solved those
great educational problems which, in their present un-
certainty, and considering their vast importance to
society, may worthily employ and well reward the
most powerful and aspiring minds. But these studies

at least form a real education, with something that may interest, something that may last, something that may set the student reflecting, and make him unwilling to live a mere life of idleness by the sweat of other men's brow. If in them, as compared with severer studies, some concession is made to the comparative feebleness of the principle of industry in those who are not compelled to work for their bread with brain or hand, it is only a reasonable recognition of the real facts of the case, to which all ideals of education, as well as of politics, must bend. The difficulties of education necessarily increase when it has to do with those who are placed by birth at the level to which other men by labour aspire, and who are heirs to wealth which they have not earned, and honour which they have not won.

One grand advantage the English system of property and society has over the rival system of the Continent,—and it is an advantage which our new scheme of education for the gentry tends directly, and we may say infallibly, to improve. The connexion between the distribution of property, especially landed property in a country, and its political institutions is necessarily close; and countries of peasant proprietors have proved hitherto incapable of supporting constitutional government. Those countries gravitate towards centralized and bureaucratic despotism with a force which in France, after many years of parliamentary liberty, seems to have decisively resumed its sway. There is no class wealthy and strong enough to form independent Parliaments, or of local influence sufficient to sustain local self-government through the country. There is nothing to stand between the people and the throne. This is the great historic service of the English landed gentry. But it is a service which cannot be well or safely performed without a political education. Europe is filled with the rivalry between the constitutional and imperialist systems, the greatest political controversy which has arisen in any age. Those who would watch that controversy with intelligence, and judge it rightly, must remember that Parliaments, like other institutions, are good as they are used. If Parliaments were to tax and legislate as ignorant and bigoted Parliaments, the blind delegates of class interests, have taxed and legislated in evil times, the case of the advocates of democratic despotism would be strong. Tyranny, the Imperialists might say, is an evil, but the worst tyranny of the worst tyrant is short, partial, intermittent, and it falls on high and low alike, or rather on the high than on the low. There is no tyranny so constant, so searching, so hopeless, no tyranny which so surely makes the people its victims, as class taxation and class law. The political ascendancy which the gentry in feudal times owed to arms they must now retain, if they retain it, by superiority of intelligence, and by making it felt that their government is a government of reason in the interest of the whole people. Conservatism itself, if it were the special function of Oxford to produce that element of opinion, ought for its own best purposes to be an enlightened Conservatism, not a Conservatism of desperate positions and ruinous defeats. We may be on the eve of social as well as political change. The new distribution of political power which all parties in the State appear to regard as near at hand, will certainly alter the character of legislation, and will very probably draw with it an alteration of those laws touching the settlement and the inheritance of property by which great estates are partly held together. In that case, Oxford may in time cease to have the same class to educate, and may have, accordingly, to qualify her system of education. But the mission of a University is to society as it is; and the political character and intelligence of the English gentry is, and will be for a long time to come, a main object of our system and a principal test of its success.

It is impossible not to be struck with the high character and the high intelligence of the English aristocracy and gentry in the early part of the seventeenth century. Their lot was cast in an evil day, when the deep-seated and long-festering division between Anglo-Catholicism and Protestantism, and between the political tendencies congenial to each, was destined, almost inevitably, to break out in a civil contest. But in that contest the gentlemen of England bore themselves so that their country has reason to be proud of them for ever. Nothing could be more lofty than their love of principles; nothing more noble than their disregard of all personal and class interests when those principles were at stake. The age was, no doubt, one of high emotions, such as might constrain the man who best loved his ancestral title and his hereditary lands to hold them well lost for a great cause. But it appears likely that education had also played its part. The nobility and gentry as a class seem to have been certainly more highly educated in the period of the later Tudors and the earlier Stuarts than in any other period of our history. Their education was classical. But a classical education meant then not a gymnastic exercise of the mind in philology, but a deep draught from what was the great, and almost the only spring of philosophy, science, history and poetry at that time. It is not to philological exercise that our earliest Latin grammar exhorts the student, nor is it a mere sharpening of the faculties that it promises as his reward. It calls to the study of the language wherein is contained a great treasure of wisdom and knowledge ; and, the student's labour done, wisdom and knowledge were to be his meed. It was to open that treasure, not for the sake of philological niceties or beauties, not to shine as the inventor of a canon or the emendator of a corrupt passage, that the early scholars undertook those ardent, lifelong, and truly romantic toils which their massy volumes bespeak to our days—our days which are not degenerate from theirs in labour, but in which the most ardent intellectual labour is directed to a new prize. Besides, Latin was still the language of literary, ecclesiastical, diplomatic, legal, academical Europe ; familiarity with it was the first and most indispensable accomplishment, not only of the gentlemen, but of the high-born and royal ladies of the time. We must take all this into account when we set the claims of classical against those of modern culture, and balance the relative amount of motive power we have to rely on for securing industry in either case. In choosing the subjects of a boy's studies you may use your own discretion ; in choosing the subjects of a man's studies, if you desire any worthy and fruitful effort, you must choose such as the world values and such as may win the allegiance of a manly mind. It has been said that six months' study of the language of Schiller and Goethe will now open to the student more high enjoyment than six years' study of the languages of Greece and Rome. It is certain that six months' study of French will now open to the student more of Europe than six years study of that which was once the European tongue. These are changes in the circumstances and conditions of education which cannot be left out of sight in dealing with the generality of minds. Great discoveries have been made by accident; but it is an accidental discovery, and must be noted as such, if the studies which were first pursued as the sole key to wisdom and knowledge, now that they have ceased not only to be the sole but the best key to wisdom and knowledge, are still the best instruments of education.

It would be rash to urge those who are destined to be statesmen, and some here may well by birth and talent be destined to that high calling, to leave the severer and therefore more highly valued training for that which is less valued because it is less severe. But those who are to be statesmen ought to undergo a regular political education, and they ought to undergo it before they are plunged into party, and see all history, all social and constitutional questions, and all questions of legislation, through its haze. There is a mass of information and established principles to be mastered before a man can embark usefully or even honestly in public life. The knowledge got up for debating societies, though far from worthless, is not sufficient. It is necessarily got up with the view of maintaining a thesis; and even the oratory so formed, being without pregnancy of thought or that mastery of language which can only be acquired by the use of the pen, is not the oratory that will live. Nor will the ancient historians and the ancient writers on political philosophy serve the turn. The classics are indeed in this, as in other departments, a wonderful and precious manual of humanity; but the great questions of political and social philosophy with which this age has to deal,—and surely no age ever had to deal with greater,—have arisen in modern times, and must be studied in modern writers. The great problems which perplex our statesmen touching the rights of the labouring population and the distribution of political power among all classes of the people, were completely solved for the ancients by slavery, which placed at once out of the pale of political existence those whose capability of using rightly political power is now the great and pressing doubt. The problems and difficulties of the representative system were equally unknown to a State which was a city, and all whose free citizens met with ease to debate and vote in their own persons in the public place. So, again, with all the great questions that have arisen out of the relations between the spiritual and the temporal power embodied in Church and State, the duty of the State towards religion, Church establishments, toleration, liberty of conscience. So, again, with the question of the education of the people, which was a simple one when the people were all freemen, supported in intellectual leisure by a multitude of slaves. In the history of the ancient republics we see indeed all the political motives and passions at work in their native form, and through a medium of crystal clearness; but under circumstances so different that few direct lessons can be drawn. Compare any revolution of Athens, Corcyra, or Rome, its simple springs and simple passions, with the vast complexity of the motives, sentiments, ideas, theories, aspirations, which are upon the scene in the great drama of the French Revolution. New political, as well as new physical maladies are set up from time to time, as one great crisis succeeds another in the history of the world. Fanatical persecution was the deadly offspring of the Crusades; terrorism of the frenzied reign of the Jacobins. Political virtues, though the same in essence, assume a deeper character as history advances. The good Trajan forbade Pliny, as procurator of Bithynia, to persecute the Christians, because persecution was *non hujusce sæculi*, it did not become that civilized age. But how far removed is this cold and haughty tolerance, which implicitly views religion as a question of police, from the deep doctrine of liberty of conscience, the late gain of a world which, after ages of persecution, martyrdom, and religious war, has found—at least its higher and purer spirits have found—that true religion there cannot be where there is not free allegiance to the truth.

Two advantages the ancient historians have, or seem to have, over the modern as instruments of education. The first is that they are removed in time from the party feelings of the present day. They might be expected to be as far from our passions as they are, considering the wide interval of ages, marvellously near to our hearts. And, undoubtedly, they are farther from our passions than the historians of the present day. Yet even to those serene and lofty peaks of the old world, political prejudice has found its way. The last great history of Greece is at once a most admirable history and a pamphlet which some may think less admirable in favour of universal suffrage, vote by ballot, and mob courts of law. The history of Rome, and of the Roman Empire especially, has been so fixed on as a battle-ground, often with much irrelevancy, by the two great parties of the present day, that in France it is becoming a question of high police, and writers are liable to fall into the hands of administrative justice for taking any but the Cæsarean side.

The second advantage of the classical historians is their style. Their style, the style at least of those we read here, undoubtedly is a model of purity and greatness; and far be it from us to disregard style in choosing books of education. To appreciate language is partly to command it, and to command beautiful and forcible language is to have a key, with which no man who is to rule through opinion can dispense, to the heart and mind of man. To be the master of that talisman you need not be its slave. Nor will a man be master of it without being master of better things. Language is not a musical instrument into which, if a fool breathe, it will make melody. Its tones are evoked only by the spirit of high or tender thought; and though truth is not always eloquent, real eloquence is always the glow of truth. The language of the ancients is of the time when a writer sought nothing but simply to express his thought, and when thought was fresh and young. The composition of the ancient historians is a model of simple narrative, for the imitation of all time. But if they told their tale so simply it was partly because they had a simple tale to tell. Such themes as Latin Christianity, European Civilization, the History of the Reformation, the History of Europe during the French Revolution, are not so easily reduced to the proportions of artistic beauty, nor are the passions they excite so easily calmed to the serenity of Sophoclean art. My friend the Professor of Poetry may be right in saying that our great age of art, in history at least, is not yet fully come.

The subject of the decline of Feudalism and the Papacy and the rise of Modern Society is not yet rounded off. The picture of that long struggle may be painted by a calm hand when the struggle itself is done. But not all ancients are classics. The clumsiest and most prolix of modern writers need not fear comparison with Dionysius Halicarnassus, nor the dryest and most lifeless with the Hellenics. Nor are all moderns devoid of classical beauty. No narrative so complicated was ever conducted with so much skill and unity as that of Lord Macaulay. No historical painting ever was so vivid as that which lures the reader through all that is extravagant in Carlyle. Gibbon's shallow and satirical view of the Church and Churchmen has made him miss the grand action and the grand actors on the stage. But turn to the style and structure of his great work, its condensed thought, its lofty and sustained diction, its luminous grandeur and august proportions, reared as it is out of a heap of materials the most confused and mean ; and ask of what Greek or Roman edifice, however classical, it is not the peer? In all those sad pages of the history of Oxford there is none sadder than the page which records the student-life of Gibbon. The Oxford of that day is not the Oxford of ours, and we need not fear once and again to speak of it with freedom. But to Oxford are, at least, partly due those foul words and images of evil which will for ever meet the eye of the historical student, passing, as the historical students of all time will pass, over that stately and undecaying arch which spans the chaos of the declining empire from the old world to the new.

The intrinsic value of studies is a distinct thing

from their educational value; though, in the case of manly education, the one, as I have ventured to submit, is deeply affected by the other. It would appear that to be available for the higher education a subject must be traversed by principles and capable of method; it must be either a science or a philosophy, not a mere mass of facts without principle or law. In my next lecture I shall venture to offer some reasons for believing, in despite of theories which seem in the ascendant, that history can never be a science. It is, however, fast becoming a philosophy, having for its basis the tendencies of our social nature, and for the objects of its research the correlation of events, the march of human progress in the race and in the separate nations, and the effects, good or evil, of all the various influences which from age to age have been brought to bear on the character, mind, and condition of man. This process is being now rapidly carried on through the researches of various schools of speculators on history, from the metaphysical school of Hegel to the positivist school of Comte; researches which, though they may be often, though they may hitherto always have been made under the perverse guidance of theories more or less onesided, crude, or fantastic, are yet finding a chemistry through their alchemy, and bringing out with their heap of dross grain after grain of sterling gold. Pending the completion of this process, or its approach to completion, I venture to think the History School must draw largely for its educational value on the two sciences (they should rather be called philosophies) which are associated with History in the School, Jurisprudence and Political Economy.

The forms and practice of the law, the art of the

advocate, cannot be studied at a University. Jurisprudence may be and is studied in Universities. In
ours, where its shade still hovers, it once flourished
so high as to threaten less lucrative though more
spiritual studies with extinction, and pointed the
high road of ambition to medieval youth. The Viner
foundation seems to have been intended to restore its
energy by the life-giving virtue of practical utility.
But there is evidence that the Viner foundation, like
that of Modern History and Modern Languages, was
received with some jealousy as an intruder on the old
studies, and it failed of its effect. Otherwise Oxford,
perchance, might have had a greater part in that code
of the laws of free England which is now beginning to
be framed, and which will go forth, instinct with the
spirit of English justice, to contend for the allegiance of Europe with the Imperial code of France.
In international law we have had the great name of
Stowell, the genuine offspring, in some measure, of
studies pursued here. The great subject of international law was once connected with my Chair. It
is now, happily, in separate hands ; and in those hands
it is united with diplomacy ; an auspicious conjunc-
tion, if we may hope that a school of diplomatists will
hence arise to raise diplomacy for ever above that
system of chicanery and intrigue of which Talleyrand
was the evil deity, and make it the instrument of
international justice. Truly great men have always
been frank and honest negotiators, and frank and
honest negotiation alone becomes a truly great people.
" He had no foreign policy," says a French statesman
of a great English minister, " but peace, good-will,
and justice among nations." A really good and impartial manual of international law is a work still to

be produced. There is the same want of a good manual of the principles of jurisprudence ; the principles of jurisprudence in the abstract, and the comparative jurisprudence of different nations. For want of this, we are driven to study some national system of law, either that of the Romans or of our own country. That of the Romans is somewhat remote, and sometimes veils its principles in forms difficult to pierce, except to a student versed in Roman history. Our own is, as yet, in form barbarous and undigested. But except in so far as it is really, and not only in forms and terms, a relic of feudalism, it covers strong rules of utility and justice, the work of the greatest and most upright tribunals the world ever saw. It is these rules, and not the technicalities or antiquities of English law, that form the proper subject of that part of our examinations ; especially as of those who pass through the School, fewer probably will be destined for the actual profession of the law, than to be county magistrates, and administer plain justice to the people.

Political Economy, though once accepted by the University as one of the regular subjects of this Chair, has but one foot, as it were, in the new Examination Statute. The candidates are permitted to include among their subjects the great work of Adam Smith. Few will think that the bounds of safe discretion are exceeded by the permission to know something of Political Economy, thus accorded to students destined, many of them from their birth, more by their wealth or talent, to become the legislators of a great commercial country ; and whose errors in economy may bring dearth of bread into every cottage, and with dearth the evils that arise

when parent and child cannot both be fed. Political
Economy is still the object of antipathies, excusable
but unfounded. A hypothetical science, true in the
abstract, but not applicable in its rigour to facts, it
has been sometimes too rigorously applied; and errors,
I believe they are now admitted to be errors, touching
the relative laws of population and food, though they
originated with minds animated by a sincere love of
man, seemed to accuse the providence and contradict
the designs of God. Political Economy is guilty of
seeking to put an end to the existence of a pauper
class. Such a class may in imagination be the kneel-
ing and grateful crowd in the picture, among whom
St. Martin divides his cloak ; imagination may even
endow them with finer moral perceptions than those
of other men ; but in the reality they are the Lazza-
roni who sacked and burned with Massaniello, and the
Sans-culottes who butchered with Robespierre. Political Economy, again, is guilty,—not she alone is guilty,
—of pronouncing that man must eat his bread in the
sweat of his own brow : she is not guilty of denying
alms to the helpless and the destitute. "Dr. Adam
Smith's conduct in private life," says the author of
the sketch prefixed to his great work, " did not belie
the generous principles inculcated in his works. He
was in the habit of allotting a considerable part of his
income to offices of secret charity. Mr. Stewart men-
tions that he had been made acquainted with some
very affecting instances of his beneficence. They
were all, he observes, on a scale much beyond what
might have been expected from his fortune; and were
accompanied with circumstances equally honorable to
the delicacy of his feelings and the liberality of his
heart." It is false sentiment to talk of a Political

Economist as though he were a religious teacher, but through no sermons does the spirit of true humanity breathe stronger than through the writings of Adam Smith; nor has any man in his way more effectually preached peace and good-will on earth. Neither his voice nor that of any teacher can put mercy into the heart of fanaticism or ambition; but his spirit always wrestles, and wrestles hard and long, with those spirits of cruelty to save the world from war. Again, no rich man need fear that he will learn from Political Economy the moral sophism that luxury may be laudably indulged in because it is good for trade. On the contrary, he will learn to distinguish between productive and unproductive labour, and the results of each to the community; and he will have it brought home to his mind more effectually perhaps than by any rhetoric, that if he does live in luxury and indolence, he is a burden to the earth. The words, "I give alms best by spending largely," have indeed been uttered, and they came from a hard, gross heart. But it was the heart not of a Political Economist, but of a Most Christian King. Those words were the answer of Louis XIV. to Madame de Maintenon, when she asked him for alms to relieve the misery of the people; that people whom the ambition and fanaticism of their monarch had burdened with a colossal debt, brought to the verge, and beyond the verge, of famine, and forced to pour out their blood like water on a hundred fields that heresy and democracy might be extirpated, and that the one true religion and the divine pattern of government might be preached to all nations with fire and sword. Once more, it is supposed that Political Economy sanctions hard dealings between class and class, and between

man and man ; that it encourages the capitalist to
use men as " hands," without fellow-feeling and
without mercy; and these charges are found side
by side with the sentimental praise of that atrocious
system of vagrancy laws and statutes of labourers by
which expiring feudalism strove to bind again its
fetters on the half-emancipated serf. The poetry of
the whip, the branding-iron and the gibbet, to be
applied to the labourer wandering to a better market,
certainly finds as little response in the dry mind of
Political Economy as the poetry of bloody perse-
cutions and judicial murder. But those who wish to
find a condemnation of the inhumanity as well as the
folly of overworking and underfeeding the labourer,
will not have far to seek it in the pages of Adam
Smith. Adam Smith, indeed, condemns in the mea-
sured language of sober justice ; and he takes no dis-
tinction, such as we find always tacitly taken in
novels and poems by the troubadours of the landed
interest, between the grinding manufacturer and the
grinding landlord. But, perhaps, his sentence will not
on either account have less weight with reasonable
men. The laws of the production and distribution of
wealth are not the laws of duty or affection. But
they are the most beautiful and wonderful of the
natural laws of God, and through their beauty and
their wonderful wisdom they, like the other laws
of nature which science explores, are not without
a poetry of their own. Silently, surely, without any
man's taking thought, if human folly will only refrain from hindering them, they gather, store, dispense, husband, if need be, against scarcity, the
wealth of the great community of nations. They
take from the consumer in England the wages of the

producer in China, his just wages; and they dis-
tribute those wages among the thousand or hundred
thousand Chinese workmen, who have contributed to
the production, justly, to "the estimation of a hair,"
to the estimation of a fineness far passing human
thought. They call on each nation with silent bid-
ding to supply of its abundance that which the other
wants, and make all nations fellow-labourers for the
common store; and in them lies perhaps the strong-
est natural proof that the earth was made for the
sociable being, man. To buy in the cheapest and
sell in the dearest market, the supposed concentration
of economical selfishness, is simply to fulfil the command of the Creator, who provides for all the wants of
His creatures through each other's help ; to take from
those who have abundance, and to carry to those who
have need. It would be an exaggeration to erect
trade into a moral agency ; but it does unwittingly
serve agencies higher than itself, and make one heart
as well as one harvest for the world.

But though the philosophy of this School may, for
the present, be drawn mainly from its Jurisprudence
and Political Economy, and these will be its most
substantial studies, there is another element, which
must be supplied by simple narrative history, written
picturesquely and to the heart. That element is the
ethical element, the training of right sympathies and
pure affections, without which no system of education
can be perfect, and for want of which mere mathe-
matical or scientific training appears essentially defec-
tive. The most highly developed power of the pure
intellect, the driest light, to use Bacon's phrase, of
the understanding, will make a great thinker, but
it will not make a man. Statesmen formed by such

education would be utterly wanting in emotion and in the power of kindling or guiding it in others. They would be wanting in the aspirations which nerve men to do great things. History in this new School has to supply the place both of the ancient historians and the poets in the Classical School; and to a great extent it may do so. And perhaps it may be truly said that Oxford has some great advantages, if she has some disadvantages, for the appreciation of historical character and the ethical treatment of history, not merely as a subject of education, but as a literary pursuit; and that she may on this ground well aspire to become a great school of history. We cannot have in this seat of learning the knowledge of the world and of action which produces such histories as those of Thucydides or Tacitus, or even as that of Lord Macaulay, any more than we can have the knowledge of war which produces such a history as that of Napier. But we have in a singular degree the key to moral and spiritual character in all its varieties and in all its aspects. Oxford gives us this key partly as she is a great school of moral philosophy, partly from events otherwise most injurious to her usefulness. Large spiritual experience, deep insight into character, ample sympathies,—these at least the University has gained by that great storm of religious controversy through which she has just passed, and which has cast the wrecks of her most gifted intellects on every shore. Such gifts go far to qualify their possessor for writing the history of many very important periods, provided only that they are combined with the love of justice and controlled by common sense.

I have mentioned that the Modern Languages were once united with Modern History in this foundation.

They have now separate foundations, but the two studies cannot be divorced. A thorough knowledge of history, even of the history of our own country, is impossible without the power of reading foreign writers. Each nation, in the main, writes its own history best; it best knows its own land, its own institutions, the relative importance of its own events, the characters of its own great men. But each nation has its peculiarities of view, its prejudices, its self-love, which require to be corrected by the impartial or even hostile views of others. We are indignant or we smile at the religion of French aggrandisement which displays itself in every page of most French historians, and at the constantly recurring conviction that the progress of civilization, and even of morality in the world, depends on the perpetual acquisition of fresh territory and fresh diplomatic influence by France. Perhaps there are some things at which a Frenchman might reasonably be indignant or reasonably smile in the native historians of a country of whose greatness we may be justly, and of whose beneficent action in Europe we may be more justly, proud. Besides, in regard to our early history much depends upon antiquarian research, and antiquarian research is not the special excellence of our practical nation. So strongly do I feel that the original arrangement by which Modern History and Modern Languages were united was the right one, that I cannot refrain from expressing a hope that the expediency of restoring that arrangement may soon come under the consideration of the Council; and that one of the most flourishing and most practically useful of our departments may be completely incorporated into our system by becoming a portion of the Modern History School.

Of the importance of physical science to the student of Modern History it scarcely becomes me to speak. All I can say is, that I have reason to lament my own ignorance of it at every turn. It is my conviction that man is not the slave, but the lord, of the material world; that the spirit moulds, and is not moulded by, the clay. I believe that nations, like men, shape their own destiny, let nature rough-hew it as she will. But nature does rough-hew the destiny of nations, and the knowledge of her workings and influences as they bear on man is a most essential part of history. The next generation of historical students in Oxford will reach, by the aid of this knowledge, what those of my generation can never attain. The words of Roger Bacon to his pupil, *Tu meliores radices egeris*, ' You will strike root deeper and bear fruit higher than your teacher,' may be repeated by each generation of intellect to that which is at once its pupil and its heir.

The range of the student's historical reading here must necessarily be limited, and we naturally take as the staple of it the history of our own country. It fortunately happens that the history of our own country is, in one important respect, the best of all historical studies. To say nothing of greatness, no nation has ever equalled ours in the long unbroken continuity of its national life. The institutions of France before the Revolution are of little practical importance or interest to the Frenchman of the present day: there is almost as great a chasm of political organization and political sentiment between feudal France and the France of Louis XIV. The French Canadian, the surviving relic of France under the old monarchy, is, in everything but race and language, a widely different man from the Frenchman of Paris. But we hear of questions in our youngest colonies being settled by reference to the institutions of Edward the Confessor. The same habits of local self-government which are so much at the root of our political character now, held together English society in the county, the hundred, the parish, the borough, when the central government was dissolved by the civil wars of Henry III., the wars of the Roses, and the Great Rebellion. It fortunately happens, also, that the main interest of our history lies in the development of our political constitution. England has always been a religious country, both under the old and under the reformed faith. But she has not been the parent of great religious movements, excepting Wycliffism, which proved abortive. She has received her spiritual impulses mainly from without. That to which the mind of the nation has been turned from its birth, and with unparalleled steadiness, is the working out of a political constitution, combining Roman order with Northern liberty, and harmonizing the freest development of individual mind and character with intense national unity and unfailing reverence for the law. The present age seems likely to decide whether this work, so full of the highest effort, moral as well as intellectual, has been wrought by England for herself alone or for the world. Political greatness is not the end of man, nor is it in political events and institutions that the highest interest of history lies. But when we arrive at the region of the highest interest, we arrive also at the region of the deepest divisions of opinion and of feeling. The English constitution is accepted by all Englishmen, and its development may be traced in this Chair without treading on forbidden ground. Even with regard to this study, indeed, it is necessary for a Professor of History to warn his pupils that they come to him for knowledge, not for opinions ; and that it will be his highest praise if they leave him, with increased materials for judgment, to judge with an open and independent mind. And, happily, in studying the constitutional history of England, modern or medieval, both professor and pupil have before them the noblest model of judicial calmness and inexorable regard for truth, in that great historian of our constitution whom Oxford produced, and who has lately been taken from the place of honour which he long held among our living literary worthies, to be numbered with the illustrious dead.

In my next lecture I propose to speak of the method of studying history. In this I have ventured to plead for support and encouragement, and, what is perhaps most needed of all, proper guidance for our Modern History School[b]. I rest my plea on the fact that there is a class of students destined to perform the most important duties to society in after life, peculiarly needing education to dispose and enable them to perform those duties, and whose education as a class has hitherto failed ; a fact to which I point with less hesitation because I am persuaded that the sense of it led in great measure to the institution of the Modern History School. I do not rest my plea on any particular theory of education, liberal or utilitarian, special or universal, because no theory of edu-

[b] I confess I have been induced to publish this lecture, somewhat late and contrary to my original intention, by the hope that I may draw the attention of the University to the state of the School of Law and Modern History, left as it is without that superintendence which in its infancy it must require, and little encouraged by the Colleges,—even All Souls having apparently set aside the Parliamentary ordinance by which its fellowships are devoted to the encouragement of the subjects recognised in this School.

cation rationally based on the results of our experience, and embracing the subject in all its aspects, as to the intrinsic value of different studies, their relative effect on the powers of the mind and on the character, and the motives to industry which can be relied on in the case of each, has yet been laid before the world. Let us look the fact in the face. We in this place differ widely in our opinions respecting education ; and our difference of opinions respecting education is intimately connected with our difference of opinions respecting deeper things. In this, Oxford is only the reflection of a world torn by controversies the greatest perhaps which have ever agitated mankind. But we are all agreed in the desire to send out, if we can, good land-lords, just magistrates, upright and enlightened rulers and legislators for the English people. We are all agreed in desiring that the rich men who are educated at Oxford should be distinguished above other rich men by their efforts to tread what to every rich man is the steep path of social duty. And if we did not all vote for the foundation of a School of Law and Modern History with a view to the better education of the gentry, we are all bound to acknowledge and support it now that it is founded. It is hard to adapt medieval and clerical colleges to the purposes of modern and lay education. It is hard, too, to break through the separate unity of the college, a strong bond as it has been, not only of affectionate asso-ciation, but of duty. Yet I cannot abandon the hope that whatever steps may prove necessary to provide regular and competent instruction in Modern History and the cognate subjects, will be taken by the Univer-sity in fulfilment of its promise to the nation. I feel still more confident that the co-operation of the Colleges with the staff of the University for this purpose will not be impeded by jealousies between different orders, which were never very rational, and which may now surely be numbered with the past. We have all one work. The Professor is henceforth the colleague of the Tutor in the duties of University education. What he was in the Middle Ages is an antiquarian question. It is clear that since that time his position and duties have greatly changed. The modern Press is the medieval Professor, and it is absurd to think that in these days of universal mental activity and universal publication men can be elected or appointed by Convocation or by the Crown to head the march of thought and give the world new truth. Oxford herself is no longer what a University was in the Middle Ages. No more, as in that most romantic epoch of the history of intellect, will the wayworn student, who had perhaps begged his way from the cold shade of feudalism to this solitary point of intellectual light look down upon the city of Ockham and Roger Bacon, as the single emporium of all knowledge, the single gate to all the paths of ambition, with the passionate reverence of the pilgrim, with the joy of the miner who has found his gold. The functions and duties of Oxford are humbler, though still great. And so are those of all who are engaged in her service, and partake the responsibilities of her still noble trust. To discharge faithfully my portion of those duties, with the aid and kind indulgence of those on whose aid and kind indulgence I must always lean, will be my highest ambition while I hold this Chair.

PRINTED BY MESSRS. PARKER, CORNMARKET, OXFORD.